PUFFIN BOOKS

Heard it in the Playground

Allan Ahlberg's new collection of poems and songs adds to his continuing portrait of primary school life. Here you can meet Billy McBone and the Mad Professor's Daughter, be amazed by the Longest Kiss Contest, shed a tear for the Boy Without a Name, and sing – if you're a teacher, feeling low – the Mrs Butler Blues. Once again Fritz Wegner has supplied the perfect illustrations.

Allan Ahlberg trained as a teacher at Sunderland College of Education. After a series of jobs including postman, grave-digger, soldier and plumber's mate, he spent ten years teaching. He lives just outside Leicester with his wife, Janet, and their daughter Jessica.

Fritz Wegner was born in Vienna and came to England in 1938. He studied at St Martin's School of Art and after the war became a freelance illustrator. Since then he has worked for magazines, publishers and advertising agencies all round the world and even designed postage stamps! He has also taught art and illustration and served as an external assessor for Camberwell College of Art. Fritz Wegner now lives and works in London.

Heard it in the Playground

ALLAN AHLBERG

Illustrated by Fritz Wegner

PUFFIN BOOKS

PUFFIN BOOKS

Published by the Penguin Group
Penguin Books Ltd, 27 Wrights Lane, London W8 5TZ, England
Viking Penguin, a division of Penguin Books USA Inc.
375 Hudson Street, New York, New York 10014, USA
Penguin Books Australia Ltd, Ringwood, Victoria, Australia
Penguin Books Canada Ltd, 2801 John Street, Markham, Ontario, Canada L3R 1B4
Penguin Books (NZ) Ltd, 182–190 Wairau Road, Auckland 10, New Zealand

Penguin Books Ltd, Registered Offices: Harmondsworth, Middlesex, England

First published by Viking Kestrel 1989
Published in Puffin Books 1991
1 3 5 7 9 10 8 6 4 2

'The Question' and 'Where's Everybody?' appeared first in
Island of the Children published by Orchard Books.

Consultant Designer: Douglas Martin

Printed in England by Clays Ltd, St Ives plc
Filmset in Monophoto Photina

CONTENTS

Short Ones

Songs

Long Ones

Teacher's prayer

Let the children in our care
Clean their shoes and comb their hair;
Come to school on time – and neat
Blow their noses, wipe their feet.
Let them, Lord, **not** eat in class
Or rush into the hall en masse.
Let them show some self-control;
Let them slow down; let them **stroll**!

Let the children in our charge
Not be violent or large;
Not be sick on the school-trip bus,
Not be cleverer than us;
Not be unwashed, loud or mad,
(with a six-foot mother or a seven-foot dad).
Let them, please, say 'drew' not 'drawed';
Let them know the **answers**, Lord!

Short Ones

Registration

Emma Hackett?
Here, Miss!
Billy McBone?
Here, Miss!
Derek Drew?
Here, Miss!
Margaret Thatcher?*
Still here, Miss!

Long John Silver?
Buccaneer, Miss!
Al Capone?
Racketeer, Miss!
Isambard Kingdom Brunel?
Engineer, Miss!
Davy Crockett?
Wild frontier, Miss!
Frank Bruno?
Cauliflower ear, Miss!

The White Rabbit?
Late, Miss!
Billy the Kid?
Infants, Miss!
Simple Simon?
Here, Sir!
Father Christmas?
Present (for you), Miss!

Count Dracula?
1, 2, 3, 4, Miss!
Necks door, Miss!
Dentist's!

The Invisible Man?
Nowhere, Miss!
Almighty God?
Everywhere, Miss!
Tarzan?
Aaaaaaaaaah! Miss.
Sleeping Beauty?
Zzz, Miss.

The Longest Kiss Contest

We seen 'em in the cloakroom, Miss –
Ann Cram and Alan Owen;
Tryin' to have the longest kiss –
They had the stopwatch goin'!

On your mouths,
Get set – go!

And Alison – and Rose – and Chris!
They've been in there since play.
Tryin' to break the record, Miss –
They'll wear their lips away.

You kiss her –
It's my turn with the watch!

Ann 'n' Chris was winnin', Miss,
Till Dennis made 'em laugh.
He pulled that face, y'know – like this:
They're gonna do a graph!

Boys

Boys will be boys
But before that
They sit around in prams
In woolly hats
With sticky chins
Waiting.

Boys who used to be boys
(i.e. *old* boys)
On the other hand
Sit around in pubs
Or on the upper decks of buses
With stubbly chins
Remembering.

Boys who *are* boys
Meanwhile
Just get on with it.

Sale of Work

Who wants to buy:
Twenty sums, half right,
Two tracings of Francis Drake,
A nearly finished project on dogs
And a page of best handwriting?

Price reduced for quick sale:
Junk model of the Taj Mahal.
Delivery can be arranged.

What am I bid
For this fine old infant's newsbook
Complete with teacher's comments?

Hurry, hurry, hurry!
Brand-new paintings going cheap –
Still wet!

The Ghost Teacher

The school is closed, the children gone,
But the ghost of a teacher lingers on.
As the daylight fades, as the daytime ends,
As the night draws in and the dark descends,
She stands in the classroom, as clear as glass,
And calls the names of her absent class.

The school is shut, the children grown,
But the ghost of the teacher, all alone,
Puts the date on the board and moves about
(As the night draws on and the stars come out)
Between the desks – a glow in the gloom –
And calls for quiet in the silent room.

The school is a ruin, the children fled,
But the ghost of the teacher, long-time dead,
As the moon comes up and the first owls glide,
Puts on her coat and steps outside.
In the moonlit playground, shadow-free,
She stands on duty with a cup of tea.

The school is forgotten – children forget –
But the ghost of a teacher lingers yet.
As the night creeps up to the edge of the day,
She tidies the Plasticine away;
Counts the scissors – a shimmer of glass –
And says, 'Off you go!' to her absent class.

She utters the words that no one hears,
Picks up her bag . . .

                              and

                                        disappears.

The Answer

We're looking for the answer,
We're searching high and low.
We're doing what we can, Sir –
We really want to know.

We've ransacked desk and drawer, Sir,
Basket, bowl and bin.
We've scrutinized the floor, Sir –
You couldn't hide a pin.

We've been out on the street, Sir;
We've been up on the roof.
And even when we cheat, Sir,
This question's answer-proof.

We've cudgelled all our brains, Sir,
And still we're in the dark.
Got nothing for our pains, Sir,
Except a question mark.

We've thought ourselves to death, Sir,
With 'What?' and 'Where?' and 'Who?'
We're beat and out of breath, Sir,
So how about a clue?

The teacher tapped his forehead.
At last! the children cried.
The answer, Sir's, in *your* head ...
What a perfect place to hide.

The Question

The child stands facing the teacher
(This happens every day);
A small, embarrassed creature
Who can't think what to say.

He gazes up at the ceiling,
He stares down at the floor,
With a hot and flustered feeling
And a question he can't ignore.

He stands there like the stump of a tree
With a forest of arms around.
'It's easy, Sir!' 'Ask me!' 'Ask me!'
The answer, it seems, is found.

The child sits down with a lump in his throat
(This happens everywhere),
And brushes his eyes with the sleeve of his coat
And huddles in his chair.

I See a Seagull

I see a seagull in the playground.
I see a crisp-bag and a glove;
Grey slides on the grey ice
And a grey sky above.

I see a white bird in the playground
And a pale face in the glass;
A room reflected behind me,
And the rest of the class.

I see a seagull in the playground.
I see it fly away.
A white bird in the grey sky:
The lesson for today.

Why Must We Go to School?

Why must we go to school, dad?
Tell us, dear daddy, do.
Give us your thoughts on this problem, please;
No one knows better than you.

To prepare for life, my darling child,
Or so it seems to me;
And stop you all from running wild –
Now, shut up and eat your tea!

Why must we go to school, dad?
Settle the question, do.
Tell us, dear daddy, as much as you can;
We're really relying on you.

To learn about fractions and Francis Drake,
I feel inclined to say,
And give your poor mother a bit of a break –
Now, push off and go out to play!

Why must we go to school, daddy?
Tell us, dear desperate dad.
One little hint, that's all we ask –
It's a puzzle that's driving us mad.

To find all the teachers something to do,
Or so I've heard it said,
And swot up the questions your kids'll ask you,
My darlings – now, buzz off to bed!

First Day Back

First day back at school
Children clean and neat
New coats hang on coatpegs
New shoes shine on feet.

School hall smells of polish
Toilets smell of soap
Children meet new teachers
Faces full of hope.

Teachers give new books out
Children start new page
Up the curtain rises
On the same old stage.

Harrison's Desk

There's something in Harrison's desk.
Put your ear against it and listen.
A noise like the chewing of pencils.

Harrison invites you to look inside.
He charges 5p a peep.
You lift the lid a little, and a little more ...

A scritching, scratching somewhere at the back.
A noise like the chewing of rulers.
A peculiar movement.

There *is* something in Harrison's desk.
Harrison won't say what it is.
He says it sharpens his pencil sometimes.

He claims it helps him with his homework.
Then: a noise like an angry burp.
Look out, says Harrison, and slams the lid.

Harrison piles heavy objects on his desk.
You suspect a trick and watch him closely.
This sometimes happens, says Harrison.

A hole begins to appear in Harrison's desk.
A tiny hairy hand protrudes.
5p a peep, says Harrison, and covers it with his hat.

Harrison counts his 5p's.
You still suspect some sort of trick.
You prepare to ask for a refund.

The piled-up desk, meanwhile, begins to shake.
A stack of books collapses to the floor.
A hole appears in Harrison's hat.

Not Now, Nigel

Not now, Nigel,
It's only half-past eight.
The school's not really open –
Your request will have to wait.

Not now, Nigel,
The register is due;
Some dinner-money's missing,
And I've got a headache too.

Not now, Nigel,
Can't you see I'm on my knees?
We're trying to find the hamster
(And I think I'm going to sneeze).

Not now, Nigel,
I'd like to hear your news,
But Alice isn't well –
She's just been sick all on my shoes.

Not now, Nigel,
Claire's bent her violin,
I ought to take a tablet
(And I *need* a double gin).

Not *here*, Nigel,
The staffroom's meant for us;
Your place is in the playground
(Or underneath a bus).

Not now, Nigel,
I still feel quite unwell;
And, furthermore, it's home time –
Off you go (saved by the bell).

Not ... now, Nigel,
Though it's nice of you to call.
I'd love to ask you in
But there's a wolf-hound in the hall.

Not... now ... Nigel,
It's really time for bed.
My temperature is rising –
There's a drum inside my head.

Tomorrow I'll feel better –
Tomorrow, wait and see.
But not now, Nigel.
The *nights* belong to me!

Swimming Lessons

If we lived in the sea
Like eels or fish,
We would go to school
And have walking lessons.
We'd reach the beach,
And – nervous in the thin air –
Learn to stagger slowly
On the warm sand.

If we lived in the air
Like dragon-flies or birds,
We'd have our walking lessons
On the tops of hills,
The parapets of tall buildings.
We'd be seized by gravity,
Nervous of the lower depths
And scared of . . . unfalling.

If we lived in the earth
Like worms or moles,
We'd come to school by tunnel
In dark glasses,
Clump along like spacemen
On the planet's shell;
Perplexed by the horizon
And the rush of blood to our feet.

The Assembly

Our Father, which art in Heaven,
We are coming to assembly
In pairs
Down the corridor – Sh!

We are here, Lord,
In the hall
In rows now – Stop that, Simon! –
Singing your Golden Oldies.

Cross-legged
On the wooden floor,
Squinting past pointed palms,
We ask You to deliver us
From splinters.

A pale-faced girl
Leaves early to be sick.
A red-faced infant
Scuttles off for a wee.
Mrs Gibbs complains about litter.

Eternal God – is *that* the time?
We collect our swimming badges,
Hand in our hymn-books
And leave – Sh!

Up the corridor
In pairs
Foreveraneveraneveraneveran –
Stop that, Simon!
Amen.

Bags I

Bags I the dummy
Bags I the cot
Bags I the rubber duck
That other baby's got.

Bags I the cricket ball
Wickets and bat
Bags I the hamster
Bags I the cat.

Bags I the pop records
Hear the music throb
Bags I the A levels
Bags I the job.

Bags I the sweetheart
Lovers for life
Bags I the husband
Bags I the wife.

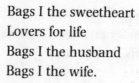

Bags I the savings
The mortgage and then
Bags I the baby –
Here we go again!

Bags I not the glasses
The nearly bald head
Bags under eyes
And the middle-aged spread.

Bags I the memories
How it all began
Bags I the grandpa
Bags I the gran.

Bags I the hearing-aid
Bags I the stick
Bags I the ending
Quiet and quick.

Goodbye world!
Goodbye me!
Bags I the coffin
RIP.

Billy McBone

Billy McBone
Had a mind of his own,
Which he mostly kept under his hat.
The teachers all thought
That he couldn't be taught,
But Bill didn't seem to mind that.

Billy McBone
Had a mind of his own,
Which the teachers had searched for for years.
Trying test after test,
They still never guessed
It was hidden between his ears.

Billy McBone
Had a mind of his own,
Which only his friends ever saw.
When the teacher said, 'Bill,
Whereabouts is Brazil?'
He just shuffled and stared at the floor.

Billy McBone
Had a mind of his own,
Which he kept under lock and key.
While the teachers in vain
Tried to burgle his brain,
Bill's thoughts were off wandering free.

Where's Everybody?

In the cloakroom
Wet coats
Quietly steaming.

In the office
Dinner-money
Piled in pounds.

In the head's room
Half a cup
Of cooling tea.

In the corridor
Cupboards
But no crowds.

In the hall
Abandoned
Apparatus.

In the classrooms
Unread books
And unpushed pencils.

In the infants
Lonely hamster
Wendy house to let;

Deserted Plasticine
Still waters
Silent sand.

In the meantime
In the playground ...
A fire-drill.

Parents' Evening

We're waiting in the corridor,
My dad, my mum and me.
They're sitting there and talking;
I'm nervous as can be.
I wonder what she'll tell 'em.
I'll say I've got a pain!
I wish I'd got my spellings right.
I wish I had a brain.

We're waiting in the corridor,
My husband, son and me.
My son just stands there smiling;
I'm smiling, nervously.
I wonder what she'll tell us.
I hope it's not *all* bad.
He's such a good boy, really;
But dozy – like his dad.

We're waiting in the corridor,
My wife, my boy and me.
My wife's as cool as cucumber;
I'm nervous as can be.
I hate these parents' evenings.
The waiting makes me sick.
I feel just like a kid again
Who's gonna get the stick.

I'm waiting in the classroom.
It's nearly time to start.
I wish there was a way to stop
The pounding in my heart.
The parents in the corridor
Are chatting cheerfully;
And now I've got to face them,
And I'm nervous as can be.

The Infants Do an Assembly about Time

The infants
Do an assembly
About Time.

It has the past,
The present
And the future in it;

The seasons,
A digital watch,
And a six-year-old
Little old lady.

She gets her six-year-old
Family up
And directs them
Through the twenty-four hours
Of the day:

Out of bed
And – shortly after –
Back into it.
(Life does not stand still
In infant assemblies.)

The whole thing
Lasts for fifteen minutes.
Next week (space permitting):
Space.

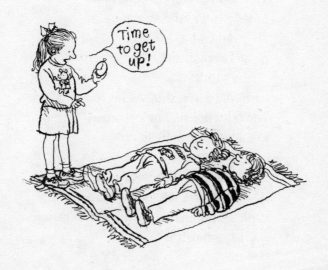

Finishing Off

The teacher said:
Come here, Malcolm!
Look at the state of your book.
Stories and pictures unfinished
Wherever I look.

This model you started at Easter,
These plaster casts of your feet,
That graph of the local traffic –
All of them incomplete.

You've a half-baked pot in the kiln room
And a half-eaten cake in your drawer.
You don't even finish the jokes you tell –
I really can't take any more.

And Malcolm said
. . . very little.
He blinked and shuffled his feet.
The sentence he finally started
Remained incomplete.

He gazed for a time at the floorboards;
He stared for a while into space;
With an unlined, unwhiskered expression
On his unfinished face.

Hide-and-seek

When we play hide-and-seek
5 – 10 – 15 – 20
And I'm on
And my eyes are shut
25 – 30 – 35 – 40
And I'm counting
And it's all quiet
Except for me
45 – 50 – 55 – 60
I sometimes think
(Just for a second)
65 – 70 – 75 – 80
Everyone's gone!
And all I'll find
Is an empty earth
85 – 90 – 95 – 100!
And just plain sky . . .

Coming-ready-or-not!

The Old Teacher

There was an old teacher
Who lived in a school,
Slept in the stock-cupboard as a rule,
With sheets of paper to make her bed
And a pillow of hymn-books
Under her head.

There was an old teacher
Who lived for years
In a Wendy house, or so it appears,
Eating the apples the children brought her,
And washing her face
In the goldfish water.

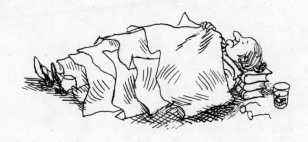

There was an old teacher
Who ended her days
Watching schools' TV and children's plays;
Saving the strength she could just about muster,
To powder her nose
With the blackboard duster.

There was an old teacher
Who finally died
Reading Ginn (Level One), which she couldn't abide.
The words on her tombstone said: TEN OUT OF TEN,
And her grave was the sandpit.
That's all now. Amen.

The Boy Without a Name

I remember him clearly
And it was thirty years ago or more:
A boy without a name.

A friendless, silent boy,
His face blotched red and flaking raw,
His expression, infinitely sad.

Some kind of eczema
It was, I now suppose,
The rusty iron mask he wore.

But in those days we confidently swore
It was from playing near dustbins
And handling broken eggshells.

His hands, of course, and knees
Were similarly scabbed and cracked and dry.
The rest of him we never saw.

They said it wasn't catching; still, we knew
And strained away from him along the corridor,
Sharing a ruler only under protest.

I remember the others: Brian Evans,
Trevor Darby, Dorothy Cutler.
And the teachers: Mrs Palmer, Mr Waugh.

I remember Albert, who collected buttons,
And Amos, frothing his milk up with a straw.
But *his* name, no, for it was never used.

I need a time-machine.
I must get back to nineteen fifty-four
And play with him, or talk, at least.

For now I often wake to see
His ordinary, haunting face, his flaw.
I hope his mother loved him.

Oh, children, don't be crueller than you need.
The faces that you spit on or ignore
Will get you in the end.

Things I Have Been Doing Lately

Things I have been doing lately:
Pretending to go mad
Eating my own cheeks from the inside
Growing taller
Keeping a secret
Keeping a worm in a jar
Keeping a good dream going
Picking a scab on my elbow
Rolling the cat up in a rug
Blowing bubbles in my spit
Making myself dizzy
Holding my breath
Pressing my eyeballs so that I become temporarily blind
Being very nearly ten
Practising my signature ...

Saving the best till last.

He's always forgetting his book

The Trial of Derek Drew

The charges

Derek Drew:
For leaving his reading book at home.
For scribbling his handwriting practice.
For swinging on the pegs in the cloakroom.
For sabotaging the girls' skipping.
For doing disgusting things with his dinner.

Also charged

Mrs Alice Drew (née Alice Jukes):
For giving birth to Derek Drew.
Mr Dennis Drew:
For aiding and abetting Mrs Drew.
Mrs Muriel Drew and Mr Donald Drew:
For giving birth to Dennis Drew, etc.
Mrs Jane Jukes and Mr Paul Jukes:
For giving birth to Alice Jukes, etc.
Previous generations of the Drew and Jukes families:
For being born, etc., etc.

Witnesses

'He's *always* forgetting his book.' Mrs Pine.
'He *can* write neatly, if he wants to.' Ditto.
'I seen him on the pegs, Miss!'
'And me!' 'And me!' Friends of the accused.
'He just kept jumpin' in the rope!' Eight third-year girls
In Miss Hodge's class.
'It was disgusting!' Mrs Foot (dinner-lady).

For the defence

'I was never *in* the cloakroom!' Derek Drew.

Mitigating circumstances

This boy is ten years old.
He asks for 386 other charges to be taken into consideration.
'He's not like this at home,' his mother says.

      The verdict

      Guilty.

The sentence

Life!
And do his handwriting again.

Songs

The music for three of these songs is traditional. 'Leavers' Song' fits 'Goodbye Old Paint', as used in the film *Shane*, and also Aaron Copland's *Billy the Kid*. 'Mrs So-and-so' fits a skipping rhyme, the title of which I forget, while 'The Grumpy Teacher' is, of course, 'The Drunken Sailor'. The idea for 'The Bell' came from the title song of *For Me and My Gal* (Meyer/Leslie/Goetz), a Judy Garland/Gene Kelly musical from the 1940s. Finally, 'The Mrs Butler Blues' can be set to almost any made-up or borrowed bluesy tune the reader (singer) feels able to get his or her throat round. Happy singing!

The Grumpy Teacher

What shall we do with the grumpy teacher?
What shall we do with the grumpy teacher?
What shall we do with the grumpy teacher,
Early in the morning?

Hang her on a hook behind the classroom door.
Tie her up and leave her in the PE store.
Make her be with Derek Drew for evermore,
Early in the morning.

Please, Miss, we're only joking,
Don't mean to be provoking.
How come your ears are smoking?
Early in the morning.

What shall we do with the grumpy teacher?
What shall we do with the grumpy teacher?
What shall we do with the grumpy teacher,
Early in the morning?

Send him out to duty when the sleet is sleeting.
Keep him after school to take a parents' meeting.
Stand him in the hall to watch the children eating,
Early in the morning.

Please, Sir, we're only teasing,
Don't mean to be displeasing.
Help – that's our necks you're squeezing!
Early in the morning.

What shall we do with the grumpy teacher?
What shall we do with the grumpy teacher?
What shall we do with the grumpy teacher,
Early in the morning?

Tickle her toes with a hairy creature.
Leave her in the jungle where the ants can reach her.
BRING HER BACK ALIVE TO BE A CLASSROOM TEACHER!
Early – in the – morning!

Mrs So-and-so

In the classroom
Sits a teacher,
Who she is we do not know.
Our own teacher's
Feeling poorly,
We've got Mrs So-and-so.

Our own teacher's
Firm but friendly,
Lets us play out in the snow.
Lets us dawdle
In the cloakroom,
Not like Mrs So-and-so.

Stop that pushing!
Stop that shoving!
Line up quietly in a row.
Somehow life
Is not the same with
Bossy Mrs So-and-so.

Our own teacher's
Kind and clever –
Not a lot she doesn't know.
Where's the pencils?
What's your name, dear?
Says this Mrs So-and-so.

Now at last
Our teacher's better
And it's time for *her* to go.
Funny thing is
Somehow we've got ...
Used to Mrs So-and-so.

The Bell

The bell is ringing
For school to begin;
The doors are open
And the children rush in.
Off they go to the classroom
Where the register's called.
Please, Miss, Paul's had a haircut!
Please, Miss, Jonathan's bald!

The bell is ringing
For playtime – what fun!
It's started drizzling
And a fight has begun.
Please, Sir, she's pinched me marbles.
No, I never! Y'did!
Please, Sir, he's smashed a window –
It'll cost him a quid!

The bell is ringing,
It's dinner time now.
I'm really famished.
I could swallow a cow!
Please don't eat like a python.
Sorry, Miss, I forgot.
Please don't talk with your mouth full.
(Please don't talk when it's not!)

The bell is ringing,
It's lessons once more.
Who's Charlotte Brontë?
What's eleven times four?
Please, Miss, Caroline's cheating.
Please, Miss, Alison's late.
Please Miss, Derek Drew's eating.
No, he isn't, he's ate!

The bell is ringing
For home time at last.
Stand clear, there's danger:
Children exiting fast.
Don't be friends with Amelia.
Let's get a gang up on Paul!
Look at Jonathan's haircut –
Like a billiard ball!

The school is silent –
No hullabaloo;
There's just the cleaners
And a teacher or two.
Cup of tea in the staffroom
Or a quick cigarette.
Making plans for tomorrow:
Can't be worse! Want to bet?

The bell is ringing
For school to begin;
The doors are open
And the children rush in . . .

The Mrs Butler Blues

I've got the
Teach-them-in-the-morning-
Playground-duty-
Teach-them-in-the-afternoon-blues.
My head's like a drum;
My feet, cold and sore.
I'm feeling so glum;
Can't take any more.
I've got the
Teach-them-in-the-morning-
Playground-duty-
Teach-them-in-the-afternoon-blues.

I've got the
Please-Miss-Tracey's-eating-
Where's-the-hamster?-
Miss-I've-broke-my-ruler-blues.
My hair's full of chalk.
There's paint on my dress.
It hurts when I talk.
My handbag's a mess.
I've got the
Please-Miss-Tracey's-eating-
Where's-the-hamster?-
Miss-I've-broke-my-ruler-blues.

I've got the
Teach-them-till-I'm-weary-
Parents'-evening-
Don't-get-home-till-midnight-blues.
I know it's a job
That has to be done,
But I'd rather rob
A bank with a gun.
I've got the
Teach-them-till-I'm-weary-
Parents'-evening-
Don't-get-home-till-midnight-blues.

One more time:
Teach-them-in-the-morning-blues.
Hmm!
How'd you like to be in my ... shoes?

Leavers' Song

Goodbye, old school,
We're going away.
Goodbye, old school,
We're leaving today.
Goodbye to the teachers,
Goodbye to you all;
The classrooms, the cloakrooms,
The playground, the hall.
Goodbye, old school,
We're going away.

Goodbye, old school,
We'll miss you a lot –
The din and the dinners,
Believe it or not.
We'll miss you, Miss,
And remember you, Sir,
When lessons have faded
And homework's a blur.
Goodbye, old school,
We'll miss you a lot.

Goodbye, old school,
We'll never forget
The smell of the cloakrooms
With coats soaking wet.
The balls on the roof
And the songs on the bus.
We'll think of you –
Will you think of us?
Goodbye, old school,
We'll never forget.

Goodbye, old school,
What more can we say?
It's *bon voyage*,
It's anchors aweigh.
The desks are quite empty;
The classroom is bare;
But our hearts are full
And you'll always be there.
Goodbye, old school,
What more can we say?

Long Ones

The Mad Professor's Daughter

She came into the classroom
In a dress as black as night
And her eyes were green as grass
And her face was paper-white.
She was tall and quite unsmiling,
Though her manner was polite.

Yes, her manner was polite
As she stood with Mrs Porter
And you never would have guessed
She was the Mad Professor's daughter.

'A new girl,' said the teacher.
'Her name is Margaret Bell.
She's just arrived this morning.
She's not been very well.'
And we stared into those grass-green eyes
And sank beneath their spell.

Yes, we sank beneath their spell
Like swimmers under water
And found ourselves in thrall
To the Mad Professor's daughter.

The sky outside was overcast;
Rain hung in the air
And splattered on the window panes
As we sat waiting there.
Our fate, we knew, was settled,
Yet we hardly seemed to care.

Yes, we hardly seemed to care,
As the clock ticked past the quarter,
That we had lost our lives
To the Mad Professor's daughter.

We did our sums in a sort of trance,
'Played' at half-past ten,
Sang songs in the hall for half an hour,
Ate lunch and played again.
And all the while, like a constant ache,
We wondered 'Where?' and 'When?'

Yes, where and when and how and why,
And what ill luck had brought her?
And whether we might yet deny
The Mad Professor's daughter.

She made no move at two o'clock.
She made no move at three.
A wisp of hope rose in our hearts
And thoughts of 'mum' and 'tea'.
And then she spoke the fatal words,
Just four: 'Come home with me!'

She spoke the words 'Come home with me'
The way her father taught her;
Her green eyes fixed unblinkingly,
The Mad Professor's daughter.

And now an extra sense of dread
Seeped into every soul;
The hamster cowered in its cage,
The fish flinched in its bowl.
We put our chairs up on the desks
And heard the thunder roll.

come home
with me!

Yes, we heard the thunder roll
As we turned from Mrs Porter
And set off through the town
With the Mad Professor's daughter.

Her silent lips were red as blood.
Her step was firm (alas!)
And the people on the street
Stood aside to let us pass.
Though this piper played no tune,
She had enthralled a whole class.

A whole class, like sheep we were,
Like lambs to the slaughter,
With PE bags and such
Behind the Mad Professor's daughter.

The rain beat down upon our heads.
The wind was warm and wild.
Wet trees blew all around us,
As up a drive we filed.
Then a mad face at a window
Stared out at us – and smiled.

Yes, a mad face at a window
That streamed with running water,
While lightning lit the sky above
The Mad Professor's daughter.

And now the end has almost come;
We wait here in despair
With chains upon our arms and legs
And cobwebs in our hair.
And hear her voice outside the door,
His foot upon the stair.

Yes, his foot upon the stair:
'Oh, save us, Mrs Porter!'
Don't leave us to the father of
The Mad Professor's daughter.

A final word – a warning:
Please heed this tale I tell.
If you should meet a quiet girl
Whose name is Margaret Bell,
Don't look into her grass-green eyes
Or you'll be lost as well.

Yes, you'd be lost as well,
However hard you fought her,
And curse until the day you died
The Mad Professor's daughter.

Kicking a Ball

What I like best
Yes, most of all
In my whole life
Is kicking a ball.
Kicking a ball
Kicking a ball
Not songs on the bus
Or hymns in the hall
Not running or rounders
But kicking a ball.

Not eating an ice-cream
Or riding a bike
No – kicking a ball
Is what I like.
Not baking a cake
Or swimming the crawl
Not painting a picture
Or knitting a shawl
Not reading a book
Or writing a letter
No – kicking a ball
Is twenty times better!

Yes, kicking a ball
Kicking a ball
With Clive and Trevor
Malcolm and Paul
Or even without them
Just me and a wall.
My legs might be skinny
My feet might be small
But I get a kick
Out of kicking a ball.

Not punching a ball
Or bashing a ball
Serving a ball
Or smashing a ball
Not throwing a ball
Or blowing a ball
Not bowling or batting
Or patting a ball
Not pinging or ponging
Or potting or putting
But booting and shooting
Yes, kicking, oh, kicking!
Just kicking a ball.

A ball in the playground
A ball on the grass
A shot on the run
A dribble, a pass
A ball before breakfast
A ball before bed
A dream of a ball
A 'kick' in the head.

Don't want a ball
That's odd or screw
That you hit with a mallet
Or a billiard cue.
Don't want a ball
That's made of meat
I'd really rather
Score than eat!
Mothballs crumble
Snowballs melt
Give me a ball
You can save – and belt!

Not a ball-cock
Or a ball-point
Or a plastic ball-
And-socket joint.
Not a ball-bearing
(Bit too small)
But – putting it more or less
Baldly – a ball.

Kicking a ball
Kicking a ball
That's surely the purpose
Of life, after all.
Not climbing a mountain
In far Nepal
Or diving for pearls
In the Bay of Bengal.
Not sailing a yacht
On a tight haul
In a sudden squall
To Montreal.
But kicking a ball
Kicking a ball
Kick, kick, kick, kick,
Kicking a ball!

And later on
As the years pass
I'll still be running
Across the grass
Kicking a ball
Kicking a ball
With Clive and Malcolm
Trevor and Paul
Not reading the paper
Or having a shave
But forcing the goalie
To make a save.
Not kissing the wife
Or bathing the baby
But kicking a ball
And scoring! (maybe)
Till baby toddles
And *tackles* and then . . .
Starts the ball rolling
All over again.

Yes, life's a circle
Endless and small
And when all's said and done
The world's a ball.

What I like best
Yes, most of all
In my whole life
Is kicking a ball.
In freezing cold
Or blinding heat
Ever and always
A ball at my feet.
Caked in mud
Covered in sweat
Scoring the goals
I'll never forget.
With Paul and Malcolm
Trevor and Clive
Completely exhausted
And *really* alive ...

And kicking, Yes, kicking
Oh, kicking!
Wow! Kicking a ball.

Schooling

Be careful of the fish tank, boys,
This gun-fighting really should stop.
I know it's a play
About old Santa Fe,
But – Alice, fetch the mop!

Don't practise your sack race in here, girls;
It's really the wrong place to hop.
Besides, can't you see
I'm drinking my tea?
And – Alice, fetch the mop!

30 kids has Mrs Butler,
Mr Jones and Mr Cutler.
All the rest have 32,
Except Mrs Pine
Who has only 29.
Still, one of them is Derek Drew –
He's worth a few!

My name is Mrs Brady,
I am the dinner-lady
And I love to see the children tucking in:
Chicken pie and chips and gravy,
Mashed potatoes, soft and wavy,
Golden pancakes served with honey,
Crisps and Coke and chocolate money,
Lots of ice-cream, lots of jelly
In each bulging little belly,
Oh, I hate to see the children looking thin.

For what they are about to receive,
Macaroni cheese or Christmas pud,
I thank the Lord and truly believe
That it will fill 'em up and do 'em good.

Je suis dans le French group.
It is bon.
Our teacher est Mademoiselle
Robinson.

In the school of life there's a teacher
Who teaches climbing trees.
His shoes are worn,
His trousers torn;
There are scabs on both his knees.

Please, Sir, please, Sir!
Give us the answers, do;
We're half crazy
Doing these sums for you.
We'd rather do them later
And we need a calculator,
So, be a toff,
Sir, let us off,
We're completely without a clue.

Please, Sir, please, Sir!
Tell us a story, do;
Lots of ghosts, Sir,
Maybe a vampire, too.
Five kids who're brave and clever,
A book that lasts for ever;
Some wolves that snarl –
By Roald Dahl! –
And a blood-thirsty ending . . . Boo!

Can I eat a cow pie?
Desperate Dan can.
Can I wear a cloak and fly?
Superman can.
Can I climb this high
Building
In the dead of night
With Fay Wray in my arms
And swat aeroplanes
From the starry sky?
King Kong can.

Can I ... take sandwiches?
The other kids can.

There's a school for clowns
I've heard about.
If you *don't* fool around
They throw you out!

There's a school for boxers
Where, it's said,
You get ten out of ten
For punching the head!

Should children be paid
For the work they do?
Is schooling a trade?
Are wages due?

Would teachers teach,
If they had to pay
The children each
A pound a day?

The teachers and the children should be friends;
I only say what good sense recommends.
Teachers like to put you right,
Children like to shout and fight,
But that's no reason why they can't be friends.

Classroom folks should stick together,
Classroom folks should get along.
Teachers, ask your questions nicely;
Kids, don't get your answers wrong!

I'd like to say a word for the teachers;
The job they do is dangerous and hard.
They all get put away
With thirty children for the day,
Except when they're on duty in the yard.

I'd like to say a word for the children;
Their little brains are bursting with ideas.
Unhappily, it's true,
The things they mostly want to do
Have been against the law for years and years.

Classroom folks should pull together,
Classroom folks should share a smile.
Teachers, put your feet up sometimes;
Children, sit still – for a while!

Boys and girls go out to play . . .
The sooner the better, the teachers say.

We're breaking up
The children shout
At breakneck speed
We're breaking out.

We're breaking down
The teachers said
We need a break
Breakfast in bed.

Who's your favourite in this class, Miss?
I like you all the same.
Yes, but – come on – who's it really?
What's his name?

Does he wear a yellow shirt, Miss?
Does his name begin with B?
Look – it's just no use your asking;
You're all alike to me.

Who's your favourite in this class, Miss?
It's impossible to say.
Yes, but you can tell *us*, can't you?
We all *know*, anyway!

Teacher loves me
This I know
For my maths book
Tells me so.
On each page
It's clear to see
Miss's kisses
Just for me.

Let the children in our care
Clean their shoes and comb their hair;
Come to school on time – and neat,
Blow their noses, wipe their feet.
Let them, Lord, *not* eat in class
Or rush into the hall *en masse*.
Let them show some self-control;
Let them slow down; let them *stroll*!

Let the children in our charge
Not be violent or large;
Not be sick on the school-trip bus,
Not be cleverer than us;
Not be unwashed, loud or mad,
(With a six-foot mother or a seven-foot dad).
Let them, please, say 'drew' not 'drawed';
Let them *know the answers*, Lord!

The teacher groans
The children shout
The cage is quiet
The hamster's out.

Heard it in the Playground

Heard
Heard it
Heard it in
Heard it in the
Heard it in the play
Heard it in the playground.

The playground
The playground
The play, the play
The playground
The playground
The play, the play.

Heard it in the playground
Heard-it-in
Heard-it-in
Heard it in the playground
Heard it in.

Heard it in the playground
Pass it to me!
Pass it to me!
Heard it in the playground
Shoot, shoot, shoot!

Heard it in the playground
Gimme my ball back!
Gimme my ball back!
Telling on you
Heard it in the playground
Telling on you.

Heard it in the playground
No I never, no I never!
Heard it in the playground
Yes you did!
Heard it in the playground
Shoot, shoot, shoot!
Gimme my ball back!
Pass it to me, pass it to me!
Heard it in the playground
Telling on you!

Heard it in the playground
Who likes bubble-gum?
Heard it in the playground
Me! Me! Me!
Heard it in the playground
I dare you, I dare you!
Heard it in the playground
Bang you're dead!
Heard it in the playground
Promise not to tell
Promise not to laugh
See this wet and see it dry
Cross your heart and hope to die
Heard it in the playground
Shick-a-boom, shick-a-boom!
Heard it in the playground
Yeah, yeah, yeah!
Me! Me! Me!
Bang, bang, bang!
Shoot, shoot, shoot!

Heard it in the playground
One potato, two potato
Heard it in the playground
Three potato, four
Heard it in the playground
Five potato, six potato
Heard it in the playground
Seven potato, more
Heard it in the playground
Seven potato, more
Eeny meeny, eeny meeny
Heard it in the playground
Meeny, miny, mo!

Heard it in the playground
Please, Sir! Please, Sir!
Heard it in the playground
Miss! Miss! Miss!
My turn! *My* turn!
His turn, her turn
Our turn, their turn
That's not fair!
Heard it in the playground
That's not fair!

Heard it in the playground
My dad says
Heard it in the playground
My mum says
Heard it in the playground
Dad says, Mum says
Cousin in the country says
Uncle in the navy says
Auntie in the army says
Auntie in the *army* says?
Auntie in the army says
Heard it in the playground
Who says? Who says?
Heard it in the playground
Sez who?

Heard it in the playground
Quality, quality
Heard it in the playground
Skill, skill, skill
Ace, nice, neat
Acely-neat
Fabby-dabby-dooby
Mega, mega, mega
Mega-dabby-dooby
Dooby-dooby-dooby
Acely-dooby
Acely-quality
Brill, brill, brill!
Skill, skill, skill!
Brill, skill, brill!
Heard it in the playground
...Wicked.

Heard it in the playground
Dog in the playground
Heard it in the playground
We'll catch him, Miss!
Leave it to us
Just watch this!
Dog in the playground
Heard it in the playground
Dog in the playground
Woof, woof, woof!

WOOF!

Heard it in the playground
I've had the measles!
Me too! Me too!
I've had it twice!
I've been to Spain!
I've got a goldfish!
We've got a new car!
We've got a newer car!
We've got a bigger car!
We've got a truck!
Heard it in the playground
We've got a truck!
85 – 90
We've got a truck!
95 – 100
We've got a truck!

5 -10 -15
20 -25 30
35 - 40 -45
50 ...

Coming-coming-coming-coming
Ready-or-not!
Heard it in the playground
Ready-or-not!
Frogspawn and caterpillars
Ready-or-not!
Heard it in the playground
Ladybird, ladybird
Heard it in the playground
Fly away home
Fly away home
Away home, away home, away
I've had the measles
The measles, the measles
We've got a truck.

Heard it in the playground
Nosy parker, nosy parker
Heard it in the playground
Boss-y-boots
Heard it in the playground
Big gob
Beanpole
Pea brain!
Pieface!
Jug ears!
Slap head!
Four eyes!
Carrot top!
Heard it in the playground
Fatty belly, fatty belly
Heard it in the playground
Bum, bum, bum
Heard it in the playground
Shick-a-bum-bum
Bum-shicka-bum
Bum-shicka, bum-shicka
Bum, bum!
Bum, bum!
Heard it in the playground
...Bum!

Heard it in the playground
Jane loves Jonathan
Heard it in the playground
That's not true!
He's your boyfriend
That's not true!
Heard it in the playground
That's not true!
You love him
I hate him!
You love him
I hate him!
You love him
I hate him!
You hate him
I love him – I
Promise not to tell
Promise not to laugh
See this wet and see it dry
Cross your heart and hope to die
Heard it in the playground
He-Man, She-Ra
Heard it in the playground
Ro-land Rat
Blue Pe-ter
Doc-tor Who
Heard it in the playground
Doc-tor Who.

East En-ders.

Heard it in the playground
Kiss chase, kiss chase
Heard it in the playground
Smack, smack, smack!
Heard it in the playground
Heard-it-in
Heard-it-in
Heard it in the playground
Heard it in.
Smack, smack, smack!
Brill, brill, brill!
Shoot, shoot, shoot!
Yeah, yeah, yeah!
Woof, woof, woof!

The playground
The playground
The play, the play
The playground
The playground
The play, the play.

Heard it in the playground
Whisper, whisper
Heard it in the playground
Pss, pss, pss!
Heard it in the playground
Please, Mrs Butler
Heard it in the playground
What shall I do?
Heard it in the playground
What shall I do?
What shall I do?
What shalla-do-shalla-do
Shalla-do-shalla
Bum-shicka, bum-shicka
Bum-shicka, bum
Pss-shicka, pss-shicka
Pss-shicka, pss
Pss! Pss!
Pss! Pss!
Pssssssssss . . .

Heard it in the playground

Heard it in the playground

Heard it in the playground

Heard it in the playground

The play-the play-the-play-the play
Ground!
The play-the play-the play-the play
Ground!
The play-the play-the play-the play
Ground!
The play-the play-the play-the play
Ground!

Heard it in the playground
What shall I do?
Gimme my ball back!
That's not true!
Heard it in the playground
Doc-tor Who!
Gimme my ball back!
Telling on you!

Heard it in the playground
Telling on you!

Heard it in the playground
Telling on you

Heard it in the playground
Telling on you

Heard it in the playground
... Telling on ...

YOU!

Author's Note

I should thank all the schools I've taught in or attended, about ten altogether. But especially I want to thank Colin Dwelly and the teachers and children of Inglehurst Junior School, and especially *especially* I want to thank Philip Fox and his class. I spent a happy year in and out of Inglehurst, watching and listening, sniffing the air (Ah, Plasticine!) ... and remembering. Every day I took home pagefuls of ideas for poems. It was like catching fish in a barrel. It was there that I saw a boy looking for the answer – up at the ceiling, down at the floor; the seagull in the playground, the wet coats (quietly steaming) in the cloakroom. Once I even found an entire 'poem' written in chalk on grey metal containers, full of school dinners, stacked up in the school yard. It went:

> Ingle jun gravy
> Ingle jun sweet
> Ingle jun veg
> Ingle jun meat!

The Longest Kiss Contest, by the way, really happened, though it was in a dormitory on a school trip, not a cloakroom in a school. So, after a fashion, did The Mad Professor's Daughter. Years ago, I had a girl named Linda Smith in my class who loved making up plays. She arranged much of my timetable around their rehearsal and performance. The Mad Professor's Daughter (more or less) was one of them. Thanks, Linda! The Boy Without a Name was a real boy, and I really can't remember his name. Kicking a Ball is three-quarters true as well; it's about me. Heard it in the Playground – the poem, not the book – is for performance (I hope). I imagine a whole classful of children belting it out.

Allan Ahlberg
August 1988

Index of First Lines

Also in Puffin by Allan Ahlberg

Don't miss . . .

PLEASE MRS BUTLER

Illustrated by Fritz Wegner

The now famous collection of verse that first introduced Mrs Butler and her school to the world.

'Hilarious and poignant verses about primary school life. A real winner' – *Guardian*

'Pick of the bunch' – *The Times*

'Fritz Wegner's pictures are a delight' – *Junior Bookshelf*

THE MIGHTY SLIDE

Illustrated by Charlotte Voake

'An absolute delight, the best Ahlberg yet' – *The Times Literary Supplement*

'The five stories in verse in *The Mighty Slide* are narrative poems to rival *The Pied Piper* and *The Highwayman*. Ahlberg never falters whether dealing with a child's experiences on a winter's day in the school playground, or with Captain Jim who gave crocodiles what for with "his bare hands and a cricket bat". Wonderful!' – *Wes Magee, Junior Education*